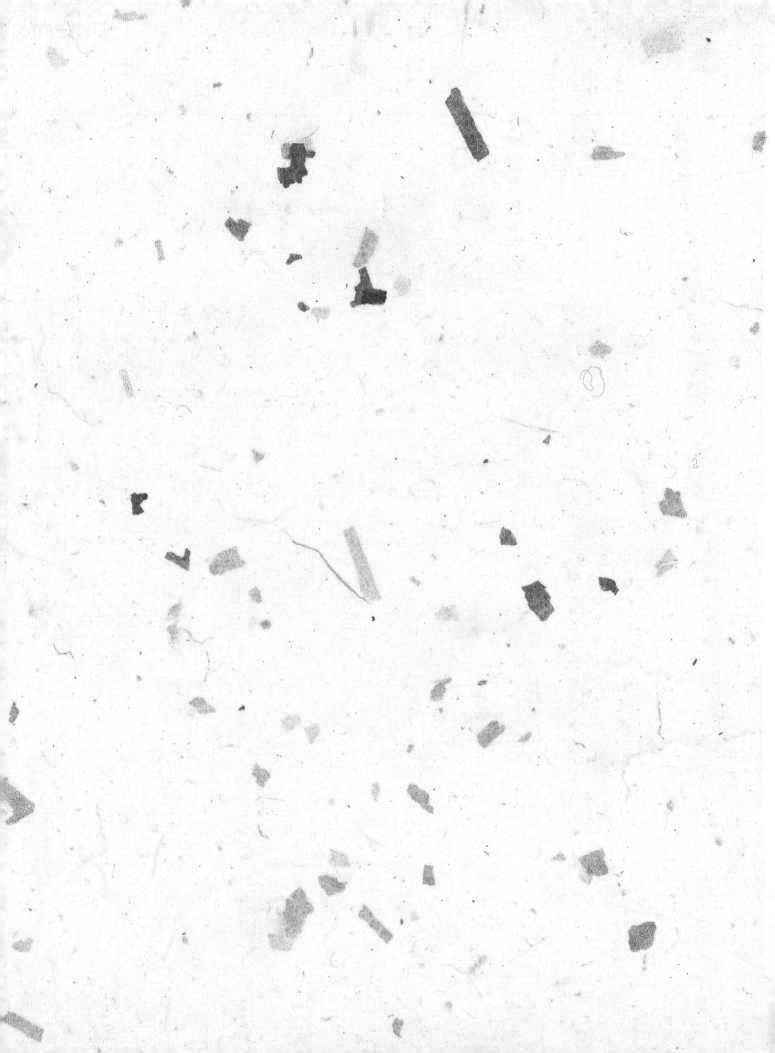

With love to my family and friends

With special thanks

to Blair Drawson

The Tiger and the Dried Persimmon is a folk tale that has been told in Korea since ancient times. My version of it comes from my grandmother, who told it to me over and over again. I have written it from memory.

I interpreted the beauty of Korean traditional shapes in my stylized illustrations using gesso, to make a unique texture on the paper, and then painting with acrylics.

— J P

Copyright © 2002 Janie Jaehyun Park

All rights reserved. No part of this book may be reproduced, stored in a retrieval system or transmitted in any form or by any means, without the prior written permission of the publisher or, in the case of photocopying or other reprographic copying, a licence from CANCOPY (Canadian Reprography Collective), Toronto, Ontario.

Groundwood Books / Douglas & McIntyre
720 Bathurst Street, Suite 500, Toronto, Ontario M5S 2R4

Distributed in the USA by Publishers Group West
1700 Fourth Street, Berkeley, CA 94710

We acknowledge for their financial support of our publishing program the

Canada Council for the Arts, the Ontario Arts Council and the Government of Canada through the Book Publishing Industry Development Program (BPIDP).

National Library of Canada Cataloguing in Publication Data
Park, Janie Jaehyun, 1965-
The tiger and the dried persimmon
ISBN 0-88899-485-0
I. Title.
PS8581.A7558T53 2002   jC813'.6   C2002-900469-1

Book design by Michael Solomon
Printed and bound in China by Everbest Printing Co. Ltd.

ONTARIO ARTS COUNCIL
CONSEIL DES ARTS DE L'ONTARIO

The Tiger

AND THE

Dried

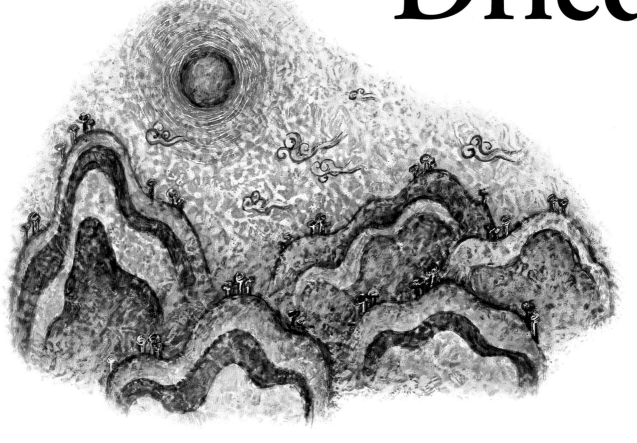

Persimmon

A Korean Folk Tale

retold & illustrated by

Janie Jaehyun Park

A GROUNDWOOD BOOK | Douglas & McIntyre
Toronto Vancouver Berkeley

Once upon a time, a big tiger lived deep in the mountains. His roar was so frightful that any animal who heard it trembled with fear. The tiger believed he was the king of all that he could see. After all, the mountains themselves almost fell down at the sound of his voice. No one had ever dared to challenge him.

But one day, the tiger made a ridiculous mistake.

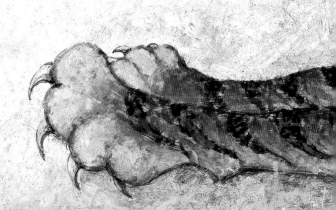

He woke up from a long nap. It was getting dark. He hadn't eaten and he was very hungry.

"Ehunggg! I am starving," he said. "I need to find something to eat."

He left his cave and began to prowl down the mountain in search of a meal. It was quite dark when he reached a small village. After roving around for a while, he arrived at a farm house. The house had a cow shed in a corner of the garden.

When the tiger sneaked into the garden, he found an ox sleeping in the shed. The ox was as big as a huge rock. "This will make a great meal! I am going to eat it for dinner tonight," he said to himself.

Just as he was about to pounce on
the ox, he heard a mysterious growling
coming from the house. He had never
heard such a sound. The tiger went
closer to the window to listen.

He saw a farmer's wife tending to a baby. The growling was coming from its mouth. The woman did not look up.

"Shhh!" she said.
Be quiet, my baby, or
we might wake up the
fierce wolf. Shhh! He's
almost here."
The baby looked
out the window for a
moment but went
right on crying.

The tiger thought, "Well, the baby is not scared of the wolf and neither am I."

Then the mother said,
"Shhh! Be quiet, my baby,
or we might wake up the big
black bear. Shhh! He's
almost here."
    The baby looked
out the window again
but went right on
crying.

The tiger thought, "Well, the baby is not scared of the black bear and neither am I."

Then the mother said, "Shhh! Be quiet, my baby, or we might wake up the fearful tiger. Shhh! He's almost here."

The tiger was sure the baby would stop crying this time. But the baby cried harder than ever.

"What a strange baby!" the tiger thought. "This baby is not scared of me at all." He was very disappointed.

Through the window he saw the mother bringing something to her baby from another room. This time the mother said, "Shhh! Be quiet, my baby, and I will give you a piece of dried persimmon. Here it is."

The baby suddenly stopped crying.

"Ehunggg!" the tiger exclaimed. "This animal called Dried Persimmon must be the meanest animal in the world." The tiger was very frightened by the dried persimmon. He decided to get as far away as he could from this dangerous creature.

But just as the tiger was slinking away, a cattle thief came sneaking up on the house. He wanted to steal the ox. He saw a great big shape looming by the window. "There's that ox," he said to himself.

Then the thief jumped onto the
tiger's back and wrapped his arms around
his neck.

"Ehunggg!" the tiger cried. "This animal on
my back must be the horrifying dried persimmon!
Now I am a dead tiger!"
He ran off as fast as he could in an effort to
shake the dried persimmon off his back.

"Amazing! I have never seen an ox run as fast as this," the thief said, holding on as tightly as he could.

On ran the tiger with the thief on his back. He ran through fields and mountains for hour after hour until finally the sun came up. The thief looked down and realized that he was sitting on the back of a tiger, not on an ox.

"Oh, my goodness! I am on a tiger! I am a dead man." The thief was so afraid that he clasped the tiger's neck tighter and tighter.

Feeling his neck being squeezed, the tiger became even more frightened. He ran faster and faster.

After a few more hours had passed, the thief noticed a low branch hanging from a big tree. He reached up as high as he could and jumped off the tiger's back.

He had narrowly escaped death and he decided never again to steal oxen from honest people.

The tiger, finally free from the terrible dried
persimmon, kept running until he reached his own cave
in the middle of the mountains. He was safe at last. He never
again went down to the village where the horrifying dried
persimmon lived.

And to this day, no one has ever seen the tiger or the thief, again.

What Is a Persimmon?

A persimmon is a fruit that is native to East Asian countries such as China, Japan and Korea. Before it is ripe, it tastes bitter, but when the fruit has ripened, it is very sweet and soft.

A long time ago people preserved persimmons to make sweet snacks. The persimmons were peeled, skewered and dried in a sunny and well-ventilated area. When they dried, a white sugary powder would form on the surface.

In Korea, dried persimmons were given to children as a sweet treat.